To my son, Walker Nathaniel Diggs. I love you.
—T. D.

Thank you, God, for always showing me ways to grow. I dedicate this
book to ALL of my family, and the "sweetness" they have shown me.
Chocolate cupcakes for you ALL!!!
—S. W. E.

SQUARE
FISH

Imprints of Macmillan
120 Broadway
New York, NY 10271
mackids.com

Square Fish books may be purchased for business or promotional use. For information on bulk
purchases, please contact the Macmillan Corporate and Premium Sales Department at
(800) 221-7945 x5442 or by e-mail at specialmarkets@macmillan.com.

Originally published in the United States by Feiwel and Friends
First Square Fish Edition: 2015
Book designed by Kathleen Breitenfeld
Square Fish logo designed by Filomena Tuosto

ISBN: 978-0-312-60326-7 (Feiwel and Friends hardcover)
10

ISBN: 978-1-250-06801-9 (Square Fish paperback)
9 10 8

AR: 2.1

CHOCOLATE me!

by

TAYE DIGGS

illustrated by

Shane W. Evans

SQUARE FISH

FEIWEL AND FRIENDS
NEW YORK

Sitting on my stoop when I was five,
not like Timmy or Johnny, or even Mark.
Though I wanted a name like theirs.

71

Chocolate me

When we'd play,
they'd say,
"Look where your skin begins!
It's brown like dirt.
Does it hurt to wash off?"

Chocolate me

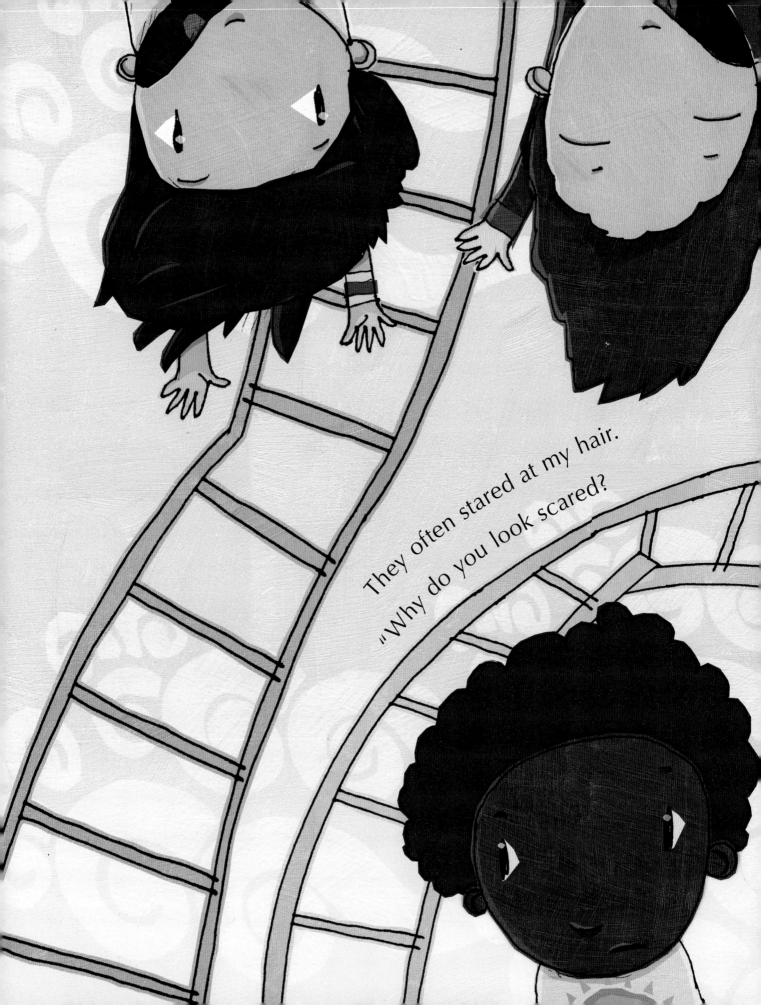

They often stared at my hair.

"Why do you look scared?

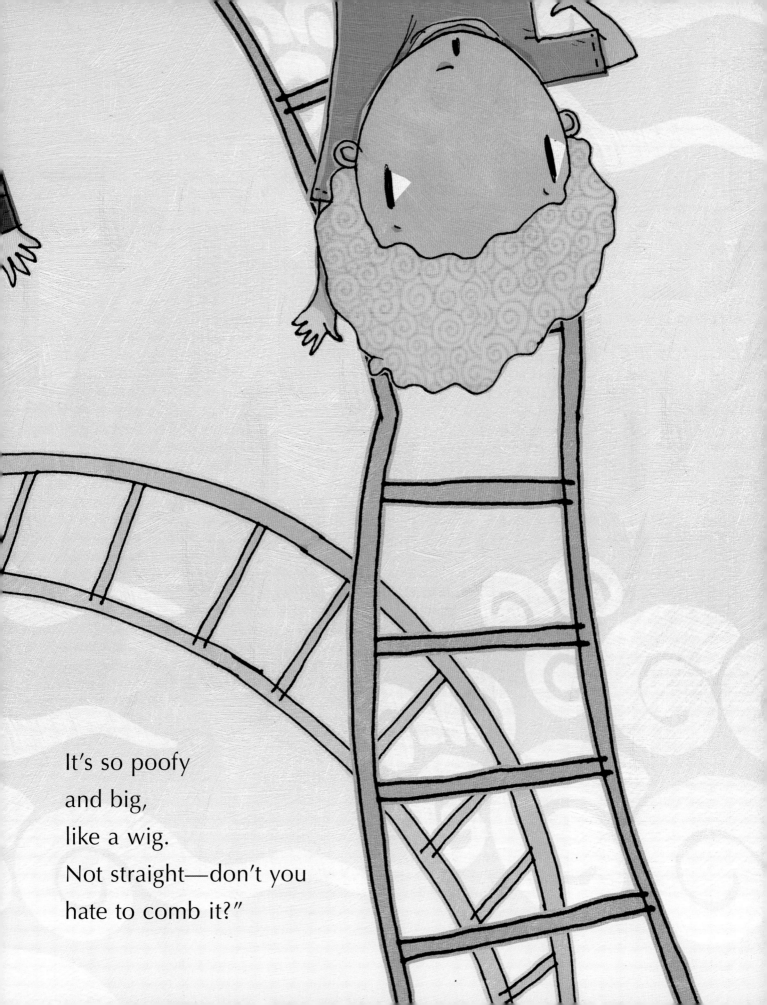

It's so poofy
and big,
like a wig.
Not straight—don't you
hate to comb it?"

Chocolate me

As they pointed at my nose,
I froze.
"It's so big and wide!"
I tried to hide.

Chocolate me

I squirmed and wiggled
as they giggled at my teeth so white.
"You can be our flashlight at night.
Just smile and we'll be alright."

Chocolate me

When I came in from outside,
I cried, "Why?"
I asked my moms,
"Why can't I be more like Timmy or Johnny or Mark
with straight hair and a different nose?
I suppose my teeth wouldn't seem so bright
if my skin were a bit more light…right?"

Chocolate me

And then my moms said,
"Wait one minute, my sweet! Can't you see?

You have skin like velvet fudge frosting
mixed in a bowl.
(You can lick the spoon.)
Cotton candy hair soft to the touch of my fingertips
or braided like rows of corn with a twist.
And your smile," she says,
"makes me so happy, I could cry.
No amount of money could buy how it makes me feel.
For real!
It's perfect."

"Look!" she says.
"Look in the mirror and
love what you see!"

Chocolate me!

Hmmmmm . . .
I started to think
about my face
my skin
my nose
my 'fro.

And what do you know?
Along came Timmy and Johnny
and Mark,
who suddenly didn't seem so smart.
And I started to smile
and smile
. . . and smile.
It felt so good, I could taste it.
Why?

'Cause I—am—**chocolate!**

Chocolate is sweet.
Chocolate is smooth.
Chocolate is beautiful and delicious.
Chocolate is—
Me!